Tiny, it will be dark soon.

Yes, Pointy.

Soon it will be very dark.

# AND THE VERY DARK DARK

by Jonathan Stutzman    illustrated by Jay Fleck

It is our first campout in the backyard,
and we are nervous.

We have never slept outside before.

We are mighty beasts.
I am a Rex, Pointy is a Pointy,
and Bob is my special squish.

But even mighty beasts get scared if we can't sleep with our nighty-lights.

When I am inside, the dark doesn't seem so dark.

But when I am *outside*, the dark is VERY dark. Outside, there are no nighty-lights to turn on.

And when there are no nighty-lights . . . the Grumbles and Nom-bies come out.

Mother says:

There's always a light shining somewhere, Tiny. Even in the dark. If you are brave and look hard enough, you will find it.

But it is hard to be brave when you are scared of the Crawly-creeps.

And it is hard to look for something when you have your eyes shut.

Pointy and I thought up a secret plan to be brave.
When the very dark dark comes, we will be ready.

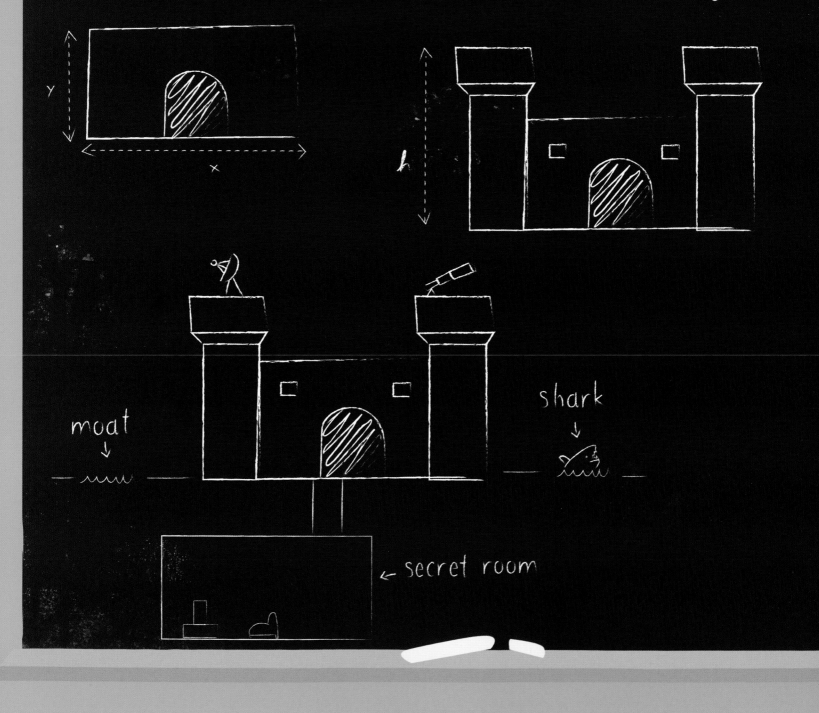

First, we will build a hiding fort.

To hide our snacks . . .

and ourselves.

*I don't feel hidden.*

Next, we will make special helmets to protect our brains from the Grumbles and Nom-bies.

*I need a bigger helmet.*

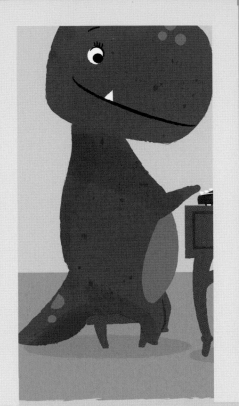

The next part of the plan is the most important. We must hurry. We are running out of time.

The Crawly-creeps are closing in.

TAP TAP TAP TAP TAP

SNNNOOOOOOORRRRE

I hear the Grumbles. They are close!

CRUNCH
CRUNCH
CRUNCH

Run, Pointy!
The Nom-bies
are here!

This is it.
Our secret plan
is almost ready.

Now we will not be scared of the very dark dark, because . . .

We have made a SUPER-BRIGHT NIGHTY-LIGHT!

Our plan did not work.

The very dark dark has got us.

I am scared. Pointy is scared. Bob is scared.
We are all scared together.

Maybe we can be brave together, too.

Brave enough to open our eyes, look very,
very hard . . .

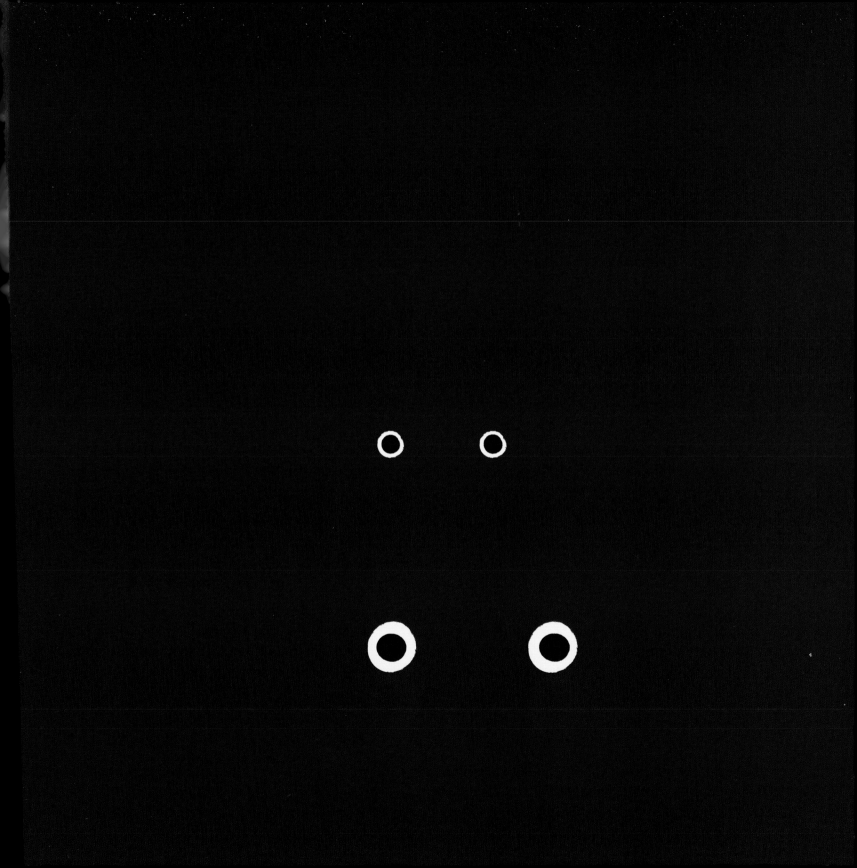

and find some light.

**For Lari, keep shining —J. S.**
**To A and O, who still sleep with the light on. —J. F.**

Library of Congress Cataloging-in-Publication Data available.

ISBN 978-1-4521-7034-3

Manufactured in China.

MIX
Paper from
responsible sources
FSC™ C104723
FSC
www.fsc.org

Design by Jennifer Tolo Pierce.
Typeset in Intelo and Brandon Printed.
The illustrations in this book were rendered in pencil
and colored digitally.

10 9 8 7 6 5 4 3 2

Chronicle books and gifts are available at special quantity
discounts to corporations, professional associations, literacy
programs, and other organizations. For details and discount
information, please contact our premiums department at
corporatesales@chroniclebooks.com or at 1-800-759-0190.

Chronicle Books LLC
680 Second Street
San Francisco, California 94107

Chronicle Books—we see things differently. Become part
of our community at www.chroniclekids.com.